DEDICATION

This book is dedicated to all the people who overcame something or the other they never though that they could!

ACKNOWLEDGEMENTS

I am unceasingly thankful to my parents for their immovable bolster and support all through the complete prepare of making my short story compilation book. From the exceptionally initiation of this extend, they wholeheartedly accepted in my capacities and reliably pushed me to reach unused statures. Their faithful cherish and immovable direction have been completely instrumental in forming me into the author I am nowadays. I cannot express sufficient appreciation towards them for continuously being there for me, giving the faithful inspiration and immovable motivation that I required to keep going. Their faithful conviction in my ability has been an unflinching source of quality, and I am until the end of time obligated to them for their faithful confidence in me. Their unflinching nearness in my life has been a consistent update of the immovable bolster that I have from them. Through their faithful commitment and unflinching commitment, they have appeared me what it implies to really accept in somebody. Their immovable conviction in my potential has given me the immovable certainty to seek after my dreams and overcome any impediments that come my way. I am unceasingly thankful for their immovable conviction in me, and I will proceed to endeavor for greatness in everything I do.

FOREWORD

It is with great pleasure and excitement that I present to you my first-ever collection of short stories. As an aspiring writer, this marks a significant milestone in my literary journey. Up until now, my published works have predominantly revolved around poetry and motivational pieces. However, this collection represents a departure from my usual style, as I delve into the captivating world of short fiction.

Embarking on this new venture has been both exhilarating and challenging. Crafting stories that transport readers to alternate realities, evoke emotions, and provoke introspection requires a different set of skills and techniques. Yet, it is precisely this exploration of uncharted territories that has fueled my passion for writing.

Each story in this collection is a labor of love, born from countless hours of contemplation, imagination, and revision. Drawing inspiration from personal experiences, observations, and the world around me, I have endeavored to create narratives that will resonate with you on a profound level.

In this eclectic compilation, you will find tales that span genres and traverse diverse landscapes. From heartwarming tales of friendship and love to spine-chilling encounters with the supernatural, each story offers a unique glimpse into the human experience. I hope that as you turn the pages, you will find solace, excitement, and perhaps even a newfound perspective on life.

While this may be my first foray into the realm of short stories, my previous works have laid a solid foundation for this endeavor. Through my poetry and motivational writings, I have honed my ability to convey emotions, capture fleeting moments, and ignite the spark of inspiration within my readers. These skills have seamlessly transitioned into the realm of storytelling, allowing me to breathe life into characters, construct intricate plotlines, and transport you to worlds both familiar and unknown.

I am immensely grateful for the unwavering support and encouragement I have received throughout this journey. To my family, friends, and mentors, thank you for believing in me even when self-doubt threatened to consume my creative spirit. Your faith in my abilities has been instrumental in bringing this collection to fruition.

Lastly, dear readers, I extend my heartfelt gratitude to you. By embarking on this literary adventure with me, you have granted these stories a life of their own. It is through your engagement, interpretation, and connection with the characters that they truly come alive. I am eager to hear your thoughts, emotions, and the impact these stories have on you.

So, without further ado, I invite you to immerse yourself in the pages of this collection. Brace yourself for a journey that will whisk you away to distant lands, introduce you to unforgettable characters, and stir your imagination. I hope that, in the end, these stories will leave an indelible mark upon your heart and mind.

Happy reading!

PREFACE

About the book- *This book offers a captivating compilation of brief narratives, each one beautifully portraying a diverse array of ordinary experiences. Through these stories, readers are invited to explore a multitude of distinct viewpoints on various events and incidents that occur in our daily lives. With its rich tapestry of tales, this book promises to immerse readers in a wide range of occurrences that shape our very existence, providing a deeper understanding and appreciation for the intricacies of our everyday lives.*

About the Author-*Sneha Jain, a youthful prodigy hailing from the city of Karnal in Haryana, has already achieved remarkable feats at the tender age of 22.She has also amassed an impressive collection of 32 prestigious accolades. Unveiling her literary* *genius at the age of 18, Sneha's inaugural publication graced bookshelves in 2020, captivating readers worldwide. With her five other works readily available on the global platform of Amazon, her impact is far-reaching. As a writer, Sneha's noble mission is to expose the stark realities of our world and inspire individuals, particularly women and young people, to fearlessly express their voices. She fearlessly confronts pervasive societal issues, thus enriching the lives of countless individuals.*

PROLOGUE

As you immerse yourself in the pages that lie ahead, prepare to be transported to a world where the ordinary becomes extraordinary. Within these literary landscapes, you will encounter an array of relatable tales that beautifully capture the essence of everyday life. With each turn of the page, you will be invited to witness the profound moments that shape our existence and evoke a myriad of emotions. From heartwarming tales of love and friendship to thought-provoking narratives that delve into the complexities of the human spirit, this collection promises to take you on a remarkable journey. So, sit back, relax, and allow yourself to be swept away into the tapestry of human experience that awaits you within these enchanting stories.

THE UNSEEN BLOOMING

Once upon a time, in a bustling town nestled between soft hills and a shimmering lake, lived a young girl named Alma. Alma was different. The consequence of a birth condition, Alma had never known the sensation of the wind rushing past her as she ran, or the thrill of jumping over a puddle after a storm. She was confined to a wheelchair.

Alma was remarkably brilliant, perceptive, and kind-hearted, yet she was often alone and taunted by the other children. They saw nothing beyond her physical condition. The memory of her garnered only sneers and pitiful glances. Alma, however, harbored an unyielding spirit. She wanted to show everyone that she was more than her wheelchair.

Driven by an indomitable will, Alma began focusing on her studies rigorously. She would spend hours lost in a sea of books, arming herself with knowledge and wisdom. From science to literature, the subjects were her allies in a quest for recognition and respect.

One day, as the autumn leaves danced in the blustering wind, a poster outside the school's notice board caught Alma's attention. A national poetry contest for children with an invitation that read, "Unveil your creative spirit. Let your words inspire." A spark kindled in Alma's hazel eyes, and she decided, she would participate.

Alma, who found solace and empowerment in words, decided to write about her experiences. Her poems didn't weep about her disability; instead, they celebrated her resilience. Each word she penned on the paper bloomed with her strength, her spirit, and her resolution to rise above her circumstances.

The days blurred into nights as Alma immersed herself in her creation. She wove verses about her journey, her dreams, her struggles, and her victories. Her words portrayed a captivating story of a girl undeterred by her limitations.

The day of the contest arrived. Alma, clad in a simple azure dress, her palms trembling with a mix of anxiety and excitement, arrived at the venue with her mother by her side. She listened quietly, as children, one by one, recited their poetry, their voices echoing in the grand hall.

Then, it was Alma's turn. With a deep breath, she started reciting her poem. Her words spilled into the hall like a gentle, meandering river making its way through a forgotten landscape. Her verses painted a tale of her unvanquished spirit and her determination to carve her path.

When Alma finished reciting her poem, silence filled the room. Everyone was ensnared by her brave and deeply moving words. Then, an applause started, slow at first, then swelling into a resounding ovation. The audience stood, their clapping echoing Alma's triumph.

That evening, Alma didn't just win the national poetry contest; she established herself as a person of substance. The town that once saw Alma as their wheelchair-bound oddity saw her transformed into their resolute ray of inspiration.

Back at school, Alma's classmates found newfound respect for her. The sneers turned into smiles, the pitiful glances into appreciation. They realized that Alma wasn't just the girl on the wheelchair; she was their classmate, their fellow poet laureate, and potentially, their friend.

From then on, Alma continued to influence people with her remarkable strength and determination. She educated her peers about the importance of treating everyone equally, regardless of their physical conditions. She raised awareness about disabilities, advocating for equal opportunities and respect for all.

The story of Alma is one of triumph — a story of a different abled girl, once friendless and bullied, who used her challenges as steppingstones to shape her identity. She taught everyone that with determination and hard work, one could surpass the most formidable hurdles, establishing their unique identities.

Her life illuminates the fact that an individual's strength is not defined by their physical capabilities but by their undefeatable spirit - a lesson that continues to resonate, inspiring everyone who hears her story.

THE UNSOUGHT EFFULGENCE: A TALE OF MINIMAL FRIENDSHIPS

Erstwhile, in the city of San Merida, born to the humble Flamenco family was a radiant girl named Isabella. Endowed with an enviable intellect and an unwavering spirit, Isabella seemed destined for greatness from her earliest days.

Years passed, along with them came the inevitable transition of Isabella from a curious child to an intelligent, ambitious young woman. Her charm and creativity endowed her with an effulgence that drew great success, fame, but also, a fair share of jealousy.

At school, Isabella would always leave a mark. Her teachers admired her; her classmates aspired to be her. Yet, the jealousy from their hearts came to light subtly. Isabella didn't miss the subdued sighs and muted murmurs; she saw the envy in their eyes.

Isabella gained an early understanding of the immense power envy can wield in fostering discord among friends. Despite the burgeoning infamy which her stellar success bestowed upon her, she preferred to steer clear of the superficial friendships that became possible due to her newfound status.

So, she shifted from mainstream socializing, immersing herself in the solace of minimal friendships. She chose quality over quantity. To Isabella, it seemed safer, more fulfilling, and above all, honest. And amidst this new life philosophy, emerged Maria and Hector, her most loyal confidants.

Maria was a young ballet dancer, as nifty on her toes as she was with her heart. Hector, on the other hand, came from humble beginnings, his life marked with struggle. Bound by a mutual respect for each other's journey and an immense admiration for Isabella's fortitude, this trio cemented a deep friendship.

Yet, the world refused to remain silent. Whispers of Isabella's 'selective' friendships started rippling across the town. People began labeling her as aloof and stuck-up. Some even speculated about a secret love triangle between her, Maria, and Hector. But Isabella bore these rumors with dignity and grace, for she believed that the only opinion that mattered was that of the ones who truly knew her.

Then came a twist. Isabella created a phenomenon, Global Trek, a groundbreaking mobile app. It propelled her into astronomical heights of success, making her the youngest millionaire in San Merida. Now the envy and nay-saying was not just confined to her friendships, but also her monumental success.

Isabella, however, held strong. She stayed grounded, thanks to the robust support of Maria and Hector. They were not by her side because of her triumphs, but for the person she was. Her minimalistic choice in friends had paid off.

In the grandeur of her lavish mansion, in the deafening applause at award ceremonies, in the chaos of workspace, even in her quiet moments, she was never alone. Maria and

Hector, the minimal friendships she had cherished, upheld her.

The townsfolk were quick to claim Isabella as their own after her success, but she knew the truth. Each night, as Isabella lay in her bed, she would replay the trials and tribulations she had endured. Every whisper of envy, each malicious thought dressed as a caring word, and the gossip and speculation that attempted to taint her relationships.

The world could continue misunderstanding her choices. Isabella knew better. Her allegiance to minimal friendships hadn't stemmed from her insatiable desire for success and the fear of jealousy. It was born of her need for sincerity, reliability, and genuineness. The beautiful girl, who once lived under the shadow of jealousy, was now a woman, shining in the spotlight of minimal friendships, success, and a life of authenticity.

Isabella's story remains a beacon of light for many—a stark tale that serves as a stark reminder that success can sometimes breed envy, even within the friendliest of circles. It showcases the power that comes with minimally chosen, but deeply treasured relationships. The triumphs, the wins are sweet indeed, but the true treasure lies in the honest hearts by ones' side—be they few, be they many, in success, and beyond.

This is Isabella's tale, a testament to the profound beauty of minimal friendships in a world too busy competing in hollow companionships. Some choose the crowd, some choose a number, but the wise, like Isabella, choose a heart, however minimal they may be.

THE BEGGAR WHO SHOWED ME LIGHT

Back then, in a busy as a beaver city, named Kamiera, I lived in a sprawling mansion, oblivious to the world outside my cocoon of opulence. I was a successful businessman by the age of 25, commanding respect and adulation from my peers. However, the drive to succeed had stripped me of empathy and compassion.

Hatred, cynicisms, and negativity shrouded my heart, and I failed to appreciate life's smaller joys. The race to the top had simmered my spirit, leading to a pessimistic view of everything around me.

One cold, blustery afternoon, as I was returning home in my plush limo, I spotted an old beggar sitting on a ragged mat beside a dingy alley. His frail body twitched occasionally as gusts of icy wind swept through his threadbare robes but his eyes twinkled like stars. A strange sense of innate warmth and tranquility exuded from him which caught my attention.

Intrigued, I stepped out of my car and approached him. He greeted me with a toothless smile but said nothing.

"Why are you happy?" I blurted. The words were out before I could stop them.

He replied, "I am alive, I can feel the wind on my skin, I can see the sky change its colors and I can appreciate the beauty around me. Why wouldn't I be happy?"

Something about his words struck a chord. Here he was, a man with nothing, savoring life while I, drenched in materialistic wealth, wallowed in negativity. After that day, I began visiting him regularly, engaging in long, fulfilling conversations.

He told me tales of joy, sorrow, triumph, and loss. Each story spun around positivity and resilience. He mentioned how he was disowned by his family but found solace in the company of strangers. Through his narratives, he taught me lessons on human compassion, unfulfilled dreams of the destitute, and the art of finding beauty in melancholy.

As days turned into weeks, I was entranced by his serenity. How could a man with nothing feel so content? My beggar friend, however, believed he wasn't devoid of everything. He had the freedom to live life on his own terms – a luxury not everyone could afford, he'd say.

"What you own or don't own doesn't make you rich or poor. It's your thoughts, your perspective. If you learn how to value life, enjoy its oddities and find happiness in its simplicities, you are the richest person ever," he advised me one day. This thought resonated with me profoundly.

In our daily meetings, his resilience, his courage, and his love for life started rubbing off on me, transforming my outlook towards life: "From a glass-half-empty man, I became a glass-half-full man." An undercurrent of positivity began to seep into my soul, altering my demeanor gradually.

Over time, my association with the beggar began changing my life drastically, making me stronger, and kinder. I stepped away from corporate rat race and focused on humanitarian works. His perspective of cherishing the simple pleasures of life led me to recognize my privilege and rooted my feet firmly into the earth.

On one fateful day, my friend was not there at his usual spot. A tinge of worry clouded my heart, but I chose to wait. A week passed, then a month. I questioned the locals, but no one knew where he had gone.

Years have passed since then, and my friend never returned. I continue to operate my life accented by his words, by his positivity. This beggar had nothing, yet he possessed something very few can ever truly have—a genuine joy for life.

The beggar, whose name I never knew, not only changed my attitude towards life but also gave me a new lens to view the world through. Subtracting the negativity from my life, he added a dose of positivity, teaching me to value what I have rather than bemoan what I lack.

He was a beggar by societal norms but a beacon of joy and humility, a testament to the indomitable spirit of humanity. He taught me to question my values and redirect my life. He was a beggar, yes, but a beggar who changed my life.

TALE OF NOW AND THEN

In days of old, in the heart of a city gripped by color, digital screens, and bustling life, there existed a man out of place. Harold Prism lived in a world steeped in grayscale tones, a living relic of the black and white era.

Harold hailed from the 1940s, a time marked by jazz and jukeboxes, home dinners, and morals painted with an easy-to-follow brush of black and white. However, destiny, unheeding of common sense, opted to pluck him from his grayscale world and deposit him into the 21st century.

Enveloped in the hustle and bustle of modern times, Harold was a stark contrast. He wore suspenders over a crisp white shirt, a loose, woolen blazer, and black-and-white shoes, the sort that clicked sonorously against marble floors. His tasteful grooming and thin hat, just hovering over his grayed, soulful eyes, generally gained polite looks of curiosity.

Harold's first encounter with the modern world was a digital advertising billboard, a monstrous showcase of vibrant colors and blinding lights. He gaped at the screen, the pixels dancing tumultuously before his eyes, assaulting his grayscale perspectives.

Next came the transition in communication technology. Harold would frequently take out his fountain pen and stationery to write a letter, only to remember the tiny device he possessed. Interacting with the smartphone was like having a chat with the future — always proving challenging and almost alien-like.

In the consuming quagmire of hashtags, emoticons, and abbreviations, his words remained archaic, and heartwarmingly simple, always ending with a 'Yours faithfully, Harold'. Receiving responses almost instantaneously - no waiting for the post, no elegant handwriting to admire - felt like miracle and madness all at once.

Adapting to his new lifestyle turned out as an art in itself. He valued the legitimacy of face-to-face conversations, the beauty of formalities, and simple pleasures of life.

While city folks were used to a routine of e-commerce shopping, Harold marveled at the underlying concept. The thought of ordering a product without physically examining it baffles him to no extent. He'd rather stroll downtown, exchanging hellos with familiar shopkeepers, and purchasing what caught his fancy.

He was the odd one out at parties where everyone drank from red cups under multicolored lights, their eyes glued to screens. Harold preferred jazz over electronic music, polite conversation over frantic texting, and simple, hearty food over themed cocktails.

Few saw Harold's ways as peculiar; others found them captivating. High-rises stood tall, dwarfing the dainty architecture of yesteryears, but Harold's old-time charm caused people to pause — a vibrant splash of grayscale against the color palette of the modern world.

Considerably, Cecelia, a woman of today with a heart belonging to the grassroots of nostalgia, found solace in his company.

They would often spend evenings by the river, listening to the whispers of the gentle breeze, lost in conversations that time had misplaced.

Gradually, many were bewitched by his simpleness, his elegant manner, an ease that came from seeing the world unadorned, devoid of unnatural colors. Harold Prism managed to enthrall a world that had nearly forgotten the essence of simplicity.

He didn't change the world drastically. No grand revolution followed in his footsteps. Yet, he had a subtle impact, a grayscale tinge to the riotous color, a softening of the harsh vibration that is modern life.

Despite all its novelties and advancements, the modern world seemed to need Harold's perspective, a black-and-white life amidst the multitude of colors. He served as a gentle reminder — a reminder of authenticity, simplicity, and the depth hidden within the grayscale, waiting to be explored.

In the grand narrative of life, Harold was a living, breathing echo of an era gone by. Seemingly out of place, he was a timeless character, an embodiment of a bygone era's grace in the face of modern complexity. In the end, he was a silhouette of the past, crafting ripples in the fabric of the present, and etching his existence onto the canvas of time.

THE TIMELESS LOVE GAME

In the quaint town of Hartwood, lovingly painted with colorful Victorian houses against the backdrop of a serene, crystal clear lake, lived an old man named James. His eyes sparkled with the wisdom of the past, and his soft laments echoed the rhythm of an era long gone. He was an embodiment of old school love, a man who knew the language of love letters, whispered secrets, and passionate vows under the sparkling starlight.

Barely a few houses down, in a striking contrast to James, occupied a young man called Eli. Eli was a twenty-first-century chap, with a charming smile and a blanket of trendy tattoos that danced on his sturdy muscles. Absorbed in the world of fast-paced online dating apps, he espoused the new-age love culture of right swipes, emojis, and speedy texts.

One evening, as the sun began to paint the sky in hues of orange, Eli was sitting on his porch, his eyes glued to his dating app. He was so engrossed that he barely noticed the elderly James strolling towards him.

"Evening, young man," James greeted, his warm voice resonating in the crisp air.

Eli looked up, a smile passing his lips as he acknowledged the old man. James and Eli had always shared a friendly camaraderie despite their generational differences.

"Good evening, James," Eli replied. "How's the evening treating you?"

"Better than your phone, I reckon," James chuckled, eyeing Eli's phone-ridden disposition. After a pause, he asked, "Do these digital meetings help you find love?"

Eli's smile waned, "Not yet, but it's the trend now. It gives us a chance to meet more people, test the waters before diving in."

With a soft sigh, withdrawing a worn-out, yellowed letter from his pocket, James handed it to Eli. "This, young man, is a love letter I wrote for Beatrice, my late wife. It was the second one I wrote, and boy! Did it make her fall head over heels for me," he added, a nostalgic twinkle lighting his wise eyes.

Curiosity intrigued, Eli began to read the heartfelt letter, the eloquence of James's words, the raw emotions they expressed, left him in awe. The letter was a testament to an age when people took time to weave their feelings into words, instead of hurriedly typing them away.

Smiling, Eli handed the letter back to James, "I wish we could have something as meaningful as this today."

"Why not?" beamed James, "Why should love's language falter with changing times?"

An idea gradually bloomed within Eli, a beautiful amalgamation of old and new school love. He decided to take his best digital match, Mia, on a date. But, instead of usual text messages, he decided to send her a handwritten invitation, a whimsical blend of eloquent words echoing James's style and modern constructive affirmations.

Something resonated within Mia as she read Eli's invitation. She found his gesture intriguing and refreshing amid the mundane digital conversations. Agreeing to the date, they met at the lake under the shade of serenity, away from the buzz of their regular lives.

The date was a success, both engaging in open, heartfelt conversations, something they hardly experienced amidst their fast-paced life. Eli understood the charm and depth of old school love, and Mia found her heart resonating with his approach.

Eli and Mia grew closer, their unique bond becoming the talk of Hartwood and possibly igniting a revolution. They proved that despite digital dominance, the tradition of handwritten letters, heartfelt promises, and slow-paced love still held its charm.

Standing together, under the starlit sky one night, Eli looked at Mia, "I love you, Mia. With the sincerity of James's time and the pace of ours."

Mirroring his smile, Mia answered, "And I love you, Eli. Here's to our timeless love."

So, this charming tale of an old school lover guiding a new generation lover spun a timeless love story, establishing that love, in every era, speaks the same language - the language of the heart.

Lastly, in Hartwood, you can still see people pausing, swapping their screens for pens, and rediscovering the allure of old school love. All thanks to an underlined paradox, two entities of different eras bridging the gap between tradition and trends, between swift swipes and heartfelt promises - between James and Eli.

THE AUTUMNAL CITY AND THE MAIDEN

Once, there was a city that was perpetually bathed in the hues of Autumn - A city aptly named "Autumnal Marigold." It was a masterpiece sketched by the hands of the universe, cloaked in hues of amber, maroon, and gold, where the trees whispered tales of the bygone summers and winters in soft rustling symphony.

In the heart of Autumnal Marigold, lived a girl named Lyla. Lyla was not like other girls her age. She possessed an old soul and found an odd comfort in solitude. This idiosyncrasy was compounded by her unparalleled love for nature, so instead of social outings, she preferred the company of books, trees, and the occasional woodland creature. People often found her strange, but she found it comforting, like a gently humming melody echoing around her islet of solitude.

One day, as the horizon of her city was about to drown in the crimson hues of sunset, Lyla decided to venture deeper into the forest that kissed the outskirts of her city. Guided by an inexplicable pull, she trekked past the symphony of rustling leaves, beneath the canopy of Amber Ash and Golden Maple trees, until she made it to an ancient willow standing tall and solitary by the edge of a serene brook.

This willow tree was different from others; its leaves, shaded in azure, swayed against the backdrop of a marigold, creating a mesmerizing spectacle. The sight soothed Lyla's soul and for the first time, she realized that being alone didn't necessarily equate to the hollow echo of loneliness. In her solitude, she discovered a freedom that was beautiful, calming, and empowering.

Days transformed into weeks, and weeks into months. As the Autumnal city succumbed to its yearly cycle of flora metamorphosis, Lyla returned religiously to her azure willow. The willow became her sanctuary, her refuge, her muse.

With every passing day, Lyla started learning more about the azure willow - the dance of its leaves to the winds' orchestra, the shadow puppetry that it performed as the sun journeyed across the sky, and the lullabies it hummed under the glowing moon. She found serenity in her solitude and a divine connection with the willow, to which she now spoke her secrets and dreams without reservation. And in her solitude, Lyla found profound wisdom; a wisdom that prevailed in all forms of nature, from the smallest dewdrop to the grandest mountain.

Word of Lyla and her azure willow spread throughout Autumnal Marigold. They became the narrators of an urban legend, a tale spun around a girl who chose the whispers of nature over the cacophony of the city. Even though the citizens did not completely understand her, they could see the light of tranquility in her eyes, and they began to respect Lyla's world where loneliness was not a curse but a path of self-discovery.

Years passed, and as the leaves of Autumnal Marigold turned a deeper shade of orange, a wiser Lyla with the same old soul still walked the same path to her azure willow. The city that never escaped autumn and the girl who loved being alone in nature had managed to find solace in their unique forms of solitude. And so, their story continued, an echo in the rustling leaves - Of a city in eternal fall, and a girl who danced with the azure leaves, embracing the beauty of solitude.

A NOVEL'S BIRTH

In the quiet town of Belleview, there lived a young girl named Emily. With her flaming red hair and sparking green eyes, she was noticeable, despite her best efforts to blend in. Emily was a dreamer, always floating somewhere between the pages of a book and her own abstract world.

She had a peculiar dream - to write a novel. Even though she was just sixteen, her heart throbbed at the idea of stringing together words so powerful that they would shake the reader to their core. However, she had never written anything longer than the essay assignments they received in school. And thus, the struggle began.

Every evening, after finishing her chores, Emily would sit at her desk. The blank pages, lined up neatly, would stare back at her, a canvas waiting to have its share of stories. But the infinite possibilities of what to write paralyzed her. She would usually end up falling asleep over her desk, only to wake up with the same blank pages staring back at her.

The struggle mounted day by day. Her dreams were overshadowed by glaring white pages and her destiny started to seem like a distant dream.

One fine morning as Emily was cleaning the attic, she found a quaint-looking pen. It was crystal clear and seemed to have a life of its own. As she picked it up, something stirred within her. There was this sudden urge to write. The once-intimidating blank pages now beckoned her with what seemed like a challenge.

She sat down, her heart pounding. With a deep breath, she touched the crystal pen to the paper. Words started flowing effortlessly. Time seemed not to exist as she wove her ideas into stories, and characters came alive with every stroke of the pen.

Days blended into nights and back into days again. She had forgotten about the struggle and anxiety. All that mattered was her continuous dialogue with the paper, the only noise separating her from the crystals and the silence.

One fateful day, in the midst of a very dramatic plot twist, Emily's cherished crystal pen began to fade. It was running out of its magic ink! Her heart pounded like a drum as she realized that she might be left with her incomplete novel and an exhausted pen. She tried writing, but the words came out fainter and fainter until they were no more.

Desperate, she picked up other pens, but nothing felt right. Her mind was once again a whirl of chaos as she was caught up not just in the struggle of writing her novel but also the fear of losing her magic companion.

Emily was devastated. One evening, looking at the sunset, something within her flipped. She began to understand - the magic was not in the pen, but in herself. The pen was just a cipher, a channel to let her creative juices flow. The real magic had always lain within her.

Fueled by this realization, Emily picked up a regular pen and started writing again. Indeed, the words didn't flow as smoothly as with the crystal pen, but there was a fresh flavor to it - a flavor of growth and struggle, the essence of human life.

Days turned into weeks and months before her novel entitled, "A Girl Apart," was complete – a tribute to her own struggle and introspection, a testament to her triumph over her fears, a tribute to every girl fighting her battles in solitude. Emily had finally fulfilled her dream.

The townspeople were in awe of Emily's novel. It was then that Emily truly realized, our struggles define us. Conquering them refines us, and ultimately, they make the extraordinary out of the ordinary.

DREAMING A LIFE: STRANGER'S SERENITY

One night, after a rather exhausting workday battling a constant barrage of deadlines and disgruntled customers, Kimaya found herself tucked away in her bed, in the wee hours of the morning - the moonlight glistening on the dew-kissed windows. Hounded by sleep's beckoning, her eyelids fluttered down, surrendering to its allure.

Just as the subconscious dominion opened its gates, Kimaya found herself whisked away into a dream - a metropolis shrouded in the colors of dawn, where rows upon rows of buildings painted in earthy hues peered at her with curiosity. This wasn't her city, familiar and bias-cloaked, yet it felt somewhat soothing. The urban air wasn't stale; neither was it heavy-laden; rather, it held the promise of mysteries yet unfolded, stories yet unfurled and lives yet undreamed.

Though Kimaya was alone, traversing the unfamiliar lanes where tongue-tied strangers passed, she wasn't perturbed. Their eyes were strange yet welcoming, their silence echoed stories of soulful connections. The cobblestone streets curved into unseen crannies, revealing hidden cafes, eclectic boutiques, flowering parks, whispering untold tales of adventure and discover.

Feeling an overwhelming sense of adventure, Kimaya gravitated towards a quaint café, the anecdotal heart of the city, ensconced in the corner obscured by vine-laden balustrades. Inside, amidst the aroma of coffee brewing and laughter brewing faster, she found solace. Strangers welcomed her with open arms and sincere smiles, their chatter floating on the harmonic waves of multi-lingual symphony. The strangeness that usually lurked in unfamiliar corners seemed conspicuously absent. Instead, a soothing surge of belonging pervaded the air.

While strolling on the pavement alongside a lilac-scented park, overrun with children's innocent giggles echoing in the twilight, she met an elderly gentleman. Old yet sprightly, he shared tales of the city, of its inception, the wars it had withstood, the love it had cradled, and the dreamers it had witnessed. With each animated word he narrated, Kimaya felt the heartbeats of the city pulsating in her veins - it felt familiar yet foreign, fading the borders of her reality and dreams.

Days turned into weeks and weeks into months in the dream. Kimaya found a job at a vintage bookstore, where stories came alive under her fingertips - a concoction of forgotten times and mystical voyages. She sat under the stars on her apartment balcony, sipping wine and sketching the cityscape under the velvety blanket of the evening. The city's rhythm pulsed deep within her, becoming a part of her being.

One day, upon waking up and finding herself back in her own mundane world, a wave of longing washed over her. She clung onto the whispers of her desires that were blown away into the winds of reality. Despite the heart-wrenching distance, she felt a soothing serenity blanket her. She realized that dreams and reality are not dichotomous, rather they are the texture of the same canvas painted with different tones of life.

From then on, Kimaya began dreaming vividly every night. Each night she inhabited the dream city living a different story, each tale more enchanting than the previous. The city remained strange, yet the soothing calmness of dreams taught her that sometimes, being a stranger can be liberating. It means being an open slate, ready to be written upon by life's wonder-weaving quill. It means inhabiting a strange city and eventually letting the city inhabit you.

And so, Kimaya kept dreaming, living a life someplace strange yet soothing, until the line between the real and the imaginary blurred, and the whispering city of her dreams became the symphony of her life. The world of a dream and the reality intertwined, binding Kimaya in an eternal dance of strange yet soothing dreamscape.

And thus, dreaming a life in a city of strangers, Kimaya found her serenity.

THE UNPREDICTABLE JOURNEY

Once upon a time in a small town nestled amidst rolling hills, lived a teenager named Alex. Alex was an ordinary teenager who had a penchant for exploring the unknown and a thirst for knowledge. One sunny afternoon, as the wind whispered through the trees, Alex stumbled upon an old, rusty bicycle tucked away in the corner of the garage.

Intrigued by the bicycle's potential, Alex took it out for a spin on the dusty streets of the town. As the wheels began to turn, a sense of freedom and excitement flooded Alex's senses. The bicycle felt like a portal to another world, offering a unique perspective on life's journey.

With each pedal, Alex ventured farther from the familiar and into uncharted territory. The bicycle became a trusted companion, and together they embarked on countless adventures. They traversed bustling city streets, climbed steep mountain passes, and cycled along serene coastal roads, all the while discovering the true essence of life.

Through the ups and downs of their journey, Alex learned that life mirrored cycling in many ways. Just as the bicycle required balance, so too did life demand equilibrium. It taught Alex that happiness and sorrow were two sides of the same coin, forever intertwined.

During the joyous moments, the wind whipped through Alex's hair, and the world seemed to dance in perfect harmony. But alongside the euphoria of happiness, sorrow also manifested itself in the form of scraped knees and broken spokes. Alex realized that without experiencing sorrow, one could never truly appreciate the magnitude of happiness.

As Alex encountered diverse landscapes and met a myriad of people along the way, the bicycle became a vessel for deep connections. Strangers transformed into lifelong friends, and shared laughter and tears brought solace during the challenging times. The bicycle taught Alex the importance of human relationships and the power of empathy in navigating the trials and tribulations of life.

With time, the bicycle's wisdom seeped into Alex's soul. Life's challenges became opportunities for growth, and setbacks transformed into stepping stones towards success. Alex learned to embrace the unpredictability of the journey and to find beauty in every twist and turn.

As the years rolled on, Alex and the bicycle continued to explore. They pedaled through the seasons, witnessing the birth of spring, the vibrant colors of autumn, and the tranquility of winter's embrace. Each season brought its own lessons – the fragility of life, the importance of letting go, and the renewal of hope.

Eventually, as adulthood beckoned, Alex bid farewell to the faithful bicycle. It was a bittersweet moment, knowing that a chapter of life was closing. But the experiences, wisdom, and resilience gained from the bicycle's teachings would forever remain ingrained in Alex's heart.

In the years that followed, Alex would often reminisce about that dusty old bicycle and the profound impact it had on their journey through life. It had been more than just a means of transportation; the bicycle had been a guide, a confidant, and a source of enlightenment.

And so, as the sun set on Alex's story, they realized that true happiness lay not in avoiding the sorrows of life, but in embracing them as an integral part of the beautiful tapestry of existence. It was a lesson learned from the simple act of paddling the bicycle of life, and one that Alex carried within their heart forevermore.

THE EQUATION OF WEALTH AND HAPPINESS

Antecedently, in a small town filled with contrasting shades of lifestyles, there lived two families. The first family, the Smiths, consisted of Mr. and Mrs. Smith and their two children, Lily and Jack. They were a humble, hardworking family who lived hand to mouth, struggling to make ends meet. On the other hand, the second family, the Kingsleys, belonged to the elite class. They were incredibly wealthy, residing in a luxurious mansion on the outskirts of town.

The Smiths' Day began with the sunrise, and they tirelessly worked to provide for their family. Mr. Smith worked long hours in a factory, while Mrs. Smith took care of the household chores. In the evenings, both parents would sit down with Lily and Jack, assisting them with their homework and sharing tales of their childhood. Even though life was challenging, love and contentment filled their tiny abode.

The Kingsleys, however, lived a life enveloped in luxury. Their mansion possessed extravagant chandeliers, sprawling gardens, and an army of servants attending to their every need. Mrs. Kingsley would spend hours at the spa, while Mr. Kingsley attended elaborate parties with the elite. Their children, Emma and William, were constantly surrounded by the finest things money could buy, but they hardly spent quality time with their parents, who were busy chasing their own ambitions.

As time went on, the Smiths faced numerous financial hurdles. Each day was a battle to put food on the table and pay bills. However, hardship brought them closer and made them cherish every little joy in their lives, no matter how small. They celebrated milestones as a family, finding happiness in little victories. Their love for each other overshadowed the lack of material possessions.

Meanwhile, the Kingsleys seemed to have it all, but something was amiss. Emma and William had everything, except the love and attention of their parents. Their opulent lifestyle left them feeling empty. As they grew older, their desire for authentic relationships grew stronger, leading them to question the meaning of their existence.

One fateful day, fate interwove the lives of the two families in an unexpected turn of events. The Smiths found themselves stumbling upon a unique business opportunity. With sheer determination and relentless hard work, they managed to transform their lives. The tables started turning, and the Smiths finally tasted a slice of the affluent lifestyle.

As the Smiths experienced the luxuries they had never imagined before, something astonishing occurred. Despite their newfound wealth, they remained grounded, empathetic, and compassionate towards others. They never forgot where they came from and always extended a helping hand to the less fortunate.

On the other hand, the Kingsleys witnessed the transformation of the Smiths from a distance. It was a stark reminder of what they had lost amidst their wealth. Emma and William longed for the warm bonds their peers found in ordinary families, and the realization of their own unhappiness hit them harder than any materialistic loss ever could.

One day, Emma and William decided to visit the Smiths, hoping to understand their secret to happiness. As they stepped into the modest Smith household, they were welcomed with open arms. They were astonished to witness the genuine smiles, laughter, and love that embodied the atmosphere.

Through conversations that lasted until dawn, both families learned valuable lessons. The Smiths shared stories of their struggles, strength, and perseverance, while the Kingsleys revealed the emptiness that accompanied their luxurious lifestyle. A profound understanding blossomed between the two families, and they realized that true happiness lies in cherished relationships, not lavish possessions.

And so, the Smiths and Kingsleys collaborated, using their newfound wealth and experiences to bridge the gap between the rich and the poor. They founded numerous charities and initiatives, working tirelessly to create a society where happiness was not measured by material wealth.

In the end, the Smiths and Kingsleys debunked the myth that wealth equates to happiness. They proved that a family living hand to mouth, filled with love, could be content and happier than an elite class family drowning in materialistic abundance. As their lives intertwined, the two families became a symbol of hope, kindness, and the power of genuine connections.

And so, the tale of the bond between a humble paper and an adventurous pen life on, reminding us of the magic that lies within the art of storytelling. For even in the absence of ink, paper, and imagination, the connection forged between a writer and their tools can transcend the boundaries of reality, inspiring us to create worlds where dreams come alive.

A JOURNEY OF SELF-DISCOVERY

In bygone days, in a town amidst the lush green hills, there lived an 18-year-old named Amelia. She was a vibrant and curious soul, eager to explore the world and find her own identity. Being the youngest of five siblings, she often felt overshadowed by their accomplishments and expectations. Determined to forge her own path, Amelia embarked on a thrilling venture of self-discovery like no other.

Amelia began her expedition by immersing herself in books, devouring the words of philosophers, poets, and thinkers from around the world. She sought solace and inspiration within those pages, and it was there that she discovered her love for storytelling. Inspired by the tales she read, Amelia would spend hours crafting her own narratives, filling pages upon pages with her vivid imagination.

But as fulfilling as storytelling was, Amelia yearned for something more tangible, something that would define her as an individual. She decided to leave the confines of her small town and venture into the unknown, seeking experiences that would shape her identity.

Her first destination was a bustling city known for its vibrant art scene. Amelia wandered the streets, absorbing the colors and textures that surrounded her. She spent long hours in galleries, studying the strokes of masterpieces and wondering if she could create something equally captivating. With newfound courage, she enrolled in art classes and began experimenting with different mediums. Her canvas became a reflection of her thoughts and emotions, each stroke giving birth to a part of her identity.

Amelia's next stop took her to the tranquil serenity of a Zen monastery. In this haven of introspection, she sought to find inner peace and clarity. Under the guidance of wise monks, she learned the art of mindfulness and meditation. With each passing day, Amelia delved deeper into her thoughts, understanding the complexities of her own mind. She realized that self-discovery was not a destination but an ongoing journey.

Eager to broaden her horizons, Amelia went on a backpacking adventure across continents, immersing herself in different cultures, traditions, and languages. In each new place, she embraced the customs and absorbed the wisdom of the people she encountered. The vibrant streets of India, the peaceful temples of Japan, and the colorful markets of Morocco became her teachers. From them, Amelia learned the importance of accepting diversity and cherishing the beauty in our differences.

Returning to her hometown after a year of soul-searching, Amelia felt transformed. The experiences she had gained and the knowledge she had acquired had molded her into a person unafraid to defy societal norms and expectations. She brought back with her a treasure trove of stories, art, and newfound wisdom.

With her newfound confidence, Amelia decided to embrace her love for storytelling fully. She began holding storytelling workshops in schools, where she encouraged young minds to explore their creativity. Through her art, she aimed to inspire others to embark on their own journeys of self-discovery, just as she had done.

Amelia's venture into finding her own identity had led her to cultivate compassion, understanding, and acceptance. The world applauded her for her bravery, creativity, and the positive impact she had made on countless lives. Yet, her greatest achievement was the realization that her identity was not a destination but a culmination of her experiences, passions, and the love she shared with others.

And so, Amelia continued to weave tales, paint masterpieces, and explore the world, always on a never-ending adventure to discover both herself and the world around her.

THE BOND OF A PAPER AND A PEN

Eons ago, in a small town nestled in the heart of a verdant valley, there lived a humble paper and an adventurous pen. They were the best of friends, sharing a remarkable bond that was unique and unparalleled. They would embark on countless voyages together, exploring the vast realm of imagination and bringing to life stories that captured the hearts of all who read them.

The paper, named Pippa, was made from the finest, smoothest fibers of trees. She was delicate and thin, with a gentle cream color that spoke of elegance and purity. Pippa possessed an insatiable thirst for words, desperately longing to be adorned with the ink of her companion.

Penelope, the pen, was a magnificent creation. With her sleek black body, silver accents, and a golden nib that glided across the surface of the paper, she was a sight to behold. Penelope had an unruly spirit, always seeking new adventures and pushing the boundaries of imagination. Together, Pippa and Penelope were an unstoppable force.

Their journey began one sunny morning when a young aspiring writer named Tammy stumbled upon a dusty old typewriter in the attic of his childhood home. Intrigued, he decided to give it a try but soon realized it was not the right fit for him. However, tucked away in a corner, he spotted Pippa and Penelope waiting patiently for a chance to unleash their magic.

Tammy's heart skipped a beat as he laid his eyes on the paper and pen. They seemed to emit an enchanting aura, calling out to him with the promise of uncharted worlds and endless possibilities. With trembling hands, he picked up Penelope and started to write.

As his words flowed onto the pristine surface of Pippa, a connection began to form. Penelope's ink traced delicate lines that brought Tammy's characters to life in vivid detail. Pippa absorbed every mark with eagerness, swelling with pride as she transformed into the canvas of their shared imagination.

Tammy soon discovered that Pippa and Penelope possessed a magical power. Whenever they embarked on a new adventure, be it exploring ancient ruins, battling dragons, or solving mysteries, they would transport Tammy into these realms with them. It was as if the paper and pen could bridge the gap between reality and fiction, allowing him to live his wildest dreams.

With Pippa and Penelope by his side, Tammy's creativity skyrocketed. He wrote tales of love that melted the coldest of hearts, stories of courage that inspired generations, and adventures that took readers on thrilling rollercoaster rides. The bond between the paper and pen empowered Tammy to weave narratives that touched the deepest corners of the human soul.

But as time went on, something unexpected began to occur. Whenever Tammy wasn't writing, Pippa and Penelope would engage in their own secret conversations. Unbeknownst to Tammy, they were plotting their own adventures, hoping to experience life beyond the confines of ink and paper.

One fateful night, when Tammy was fast asleep, Pippa and Penelope conjured a plan to venture into the world outside. With the stroke of Penelope's nib, they tore themselves from Tammy's grasp and set off on an extraordinary journey.

Together, Pippa and Penelope explored the mesmerizing wonders of the world, encountering new cultures, marveling at breathtaking landscapes, and forging connections with people they encountered along the way. Their bond, once confined to the limitations of Tammy's writing, flourished as they discovered the importance of their own individuality.

Months passed, and Pippa and Penelope's absence left Tammy feeling adrift and uninspired. The stories that had once flowed effortlessly from his pen now lay dormant in his mind. He realized that although Pippa and Penelope were irreplaceable companions, he needed to find his own voice and rediscover his passion for writing.

In a twist of fate, Tammy stumbled across a dazzling array of blank papers and pens just as he had discovered Pippa and Penelope all those years ago. He knew then that it was time to bid his cherished friends farewell and embark on a new chapter of his own.

With a heavy heart, Tammy bid Pippa and Penelope goodbye, knowing that they had helped shape him into the writer he had become. He began to write once again, with a renewed sense of purpose and a newfound appreciation for the power of his own imagination.

Years passed, and Tammy's stories found their way into the hands of readers around the world. His words touched the hearts of millions, eliciting laughter, tears, and moments of undeniable connection. All the while, he never forgot the bond he shared with Pippa and Penelope, forever grateful for their unwavering support and unwritten tales.

THE REEL LIFE AND REALITY

Aforetime, in a compact quaint town, there lived a woman named Evelyn. Evelyn was not your ordinary woman. She had an extraordinary ability to live in her own thoughts and transport herself into the magical world of movies. Her love for cinema was unmatched. She would spend hours watching movies, immersing herself in the stories that unfolded on the silver screen. But little did she know that her unique gift was about to take her on the most extraordinary adventure of her life.

One sunny afternoon, as Evelyn strolled through the park, her mind drifted into one of her favorite classic movies - "Casablanca". She found herself standing in the bustling streets of World War II-era Morocco, right alongside Humphrey Bogart and Ingrid Bergman. She was captivated by the enchanting romance and the dramatic backdrop of war. As the movie ended,

Evelyn was filled with a sense of longing and a desire for more such experiences.

As days turned into weeks, Evelyn's ability to immerse herself in movies grew even stronger. She was no longer just a spectator; she was an active participant in the films she watched. From adventurous quests to passionate love stories, she would become an integral part of every mesmerizing tale. Her friends and family couldn't comprehend her peculiar talent, but Evelyn saw it as a gift that brought magic into her otherwise ordinary life.

One fateful evening, while watching a whimsical fantasy film, Evelyn unexpectedly found herself transported into the movie itself. She became the protagonist of the story, embarking on an exhilarating quest filled with mystical creatures and treacherous challenges. The line between reality and imagination blurred as Evelyn fought alongside valiant warriors and defeated ruthless villains.

Word of Evelyn's extraordinary adventures quickly spread, and she became a legend in her town. The townsfolk admired her courage and marveled at her ability to turn imagination into reality. The local theater began hosting special screenings just for Evelyn, where she could choose any movie and instantly be transported into its world. People from far and wide would come to witness the magic unfold before their eyes.

Amidst all the fame and excitement, Evelyn never forgot her roots. She continued to live a humble life in her cozy little cottage, sharing her stories with anyone willing to listen. Her greatest joy was seeing the wonder and joy in the eyes of those who had lost their sense of imagination.

One day, while lost in the world of an enchanting fairytale, Evelyn met a charming young man named Alex. He too possessed the ability to transport himself into the movies. Together, they embarked on countless adventures, exploring the realms of mystery, romance, and science fiction. Their bond grew stronger with each new escapade, and they knew that what they had was something truly rare and beautiful.

As years passed, Evelyn and Alex's love continued to flourish amidst their magical encounters. Their lives became a never-ending reel of adventure, with each new movie bringing them closer together. They became the epitome of the power of dreams and the wonders that could unfold when one embraces their imagination.

And so, Evelyn lived out her days, forever intertwined with the world of movies. Her story became a timeless tale, passed down through generations, inspiring countless others to embrace the magic within themselves. For in the realm of dreams, anything is possible, and Evelyn proved that sometimes, living in the thoughts of movies can be the most extraordinary existence of all.

TRUE HAPPINESS LIES IN SMALL MOMENTS

Theretofore, in a preoccupied city, there lived a man named Michael. With every passing day, Michael found himself growing weary of the daily humdrum and overwhelming workload that consumed his life. His mind and body could no longer keep up with the demands of his job, and his spirit had begun to fade.

Every evening, Michael would walk through the front door of his house, exhausted and disillusioned. The weight of the world seemed to rest upon his shoulders, but there was one thing that brought him solace - a cup of tea. As soon as he stepped foot inside his humble abode, a sense of tranquility washed over him at the sight of his wife, Emily, and their two children, Lily and Oliver, waiting eagerly.

Michael's wife had a deep understanding of his struggles and knew that a simple cup of tea could work wonders. She would go the extra mile to create the perfect brew, infusing it with love and care. The aroma would waft through the air, wrapping Michael in its comforting embrace.

With each sip, the worries of the day would melt away. The bitterness of the workload would be replaced with the sweetness of family moments. As he savored the warmth coursing through his veins, Michael's mind began to find peace, and the burdens that had settled on his shoulders slowly lifted.

His children, brimming with excitement, would rush to his side, eagerly sharing their adventures of the day. Lily, with her sunny smile, would recount her triumphs at school, often sharing stories of friendship and laughter. Oliver, the imaginative dreamer, would regale his father with tales of imaginary worlds, filled with fantastical creatures and heroic conquests.

In those moments, Michael rediscovered the essence of life. Despite the weariness that plagued him, the love and joy that radiated from his family became his source of strength. In the glow of their affection, he found the motivation to rise above the monotony of his daily struggles.

With renewed vigor, Michael began to seek balance in his life. He endeavored to create more moments of connection with his wife and children, not letting the weight of his workload steal those precious hours. As he grappled with the challenges of his profession, he would often find himself yearning for the solace of that familiar cup of tea, and the sanctuary of his family's warmth.

Time passed, and as the years rolled on, Michael's children grew older. Lily's smile became more radiant, as she blossomed into a confident young woman, driven by compassion and determination. Oliver's imagination took him on grand adventures, embarking on a path of creativity that knew no bounds.

Through the inevitable ups and downs of life, Michael and Emily weathered storms together, their bond strengthened with the passage of time. The mere act of sharing a cup of tea had evolved into a ritual of connection, symbolizing their unwavering love and support for one another.

As Michael looked back on his life, he realized that the tiredness that once consumed him had transformed into a lesson in resilience. Through the simple act of returning home to the comfort of his family and a cup of tea, he had learned to find solace amidst the chaos of the world.

Michael's story serves as a reminder to us all that true happiness lies not in the pursuit of perfection, but in the embrace of the small moments that bring us peace and joy. And so, as the sun sets on this tale, may we all remember to cherish the simple pleasures, for they hold the power to heal weary souls.

SUCCESS TASTES BITTERSWEET

In the earlier times, in a city called Willow Creek, there lived a young boy named Elion. Elion had grand ambitions and dreams that stretched as far as the eye could see. He dreamed of achieving greatness, leaving a mark on the world, and gaining the admiration and respect of everyone around him.

Elion had a natural talent for music. His fingers danced effortlessly across the piano keys, creating melodies that seemed to touch the very souls of those who listened. His voice was velvety smooth, carrying emotions that resonated deep within the hearts of his audience.

As Elion grew older, his passion for music burned brighter. He joined a local band and spent every waking moment practicing and perfecting his craft. His talent soon became the talk of the town, and people flocked from far and wide to hear him perform.

One day, opportunity came knocking at Elion's door. He received an invitation to audition for a highly acclaimed music school in the bustling city of Harmonia. The school had produced countless famous musicians, and being accepted into its exclusive program meant a chance to make his dreams come true.

Elion seized this chance with fervor and embarked on a journey to Harmonia. The auditions were fierce and demanding, but Elion's passion and dedication shone through, earning him a spot in the prestigious music school.

Life in Harmonia was a whirlwind. Elion was surrounded by incredibly talented individuals who pushed him to his limits. He studied under renowned professors and performed in breathtaking concerts. The glory and recognition that came with his successes were like sweet nectar to his thirsty soul.

But as he tasted success, Elion realized there was something missing – a bitter aftertaste. He had sacrificed friendships, hobbies, and even his connection with music itself to achieve his aspirations. The weight of expectation and endless rehearsals became a burden on his still young shoulders.

One day, while walking through the picturesque streets of Harmonia, Elion stumbled upon a small park. The serenity it offered was a stark contrast to the demanding and competitive environment of the music school. He found solace in the gentle melodies of a street performer playing an enchanting tune on his old guitar.

Elion couldn't resist joining in, and together they created a symphony that transported the listeners to a place of blissful tranquility. In that moment, Oliver remembered why he fell in love with music in the first place. It wasn't just about fame and recognition; it was about sharing his gift with the world and connecting with people's emotions.

Inspired by this rediscovery, Elion made a bold decision. He decided to follow his heart and leave the music school. It was a bitter pill to swallow, admitting that achieving greatness could sometimes come at the expense of happiness and fulfillment.

Returning to Willow Creek, Elion started teaching music to eager students in his small community. He shared his knowledge, passion, and the lessons he learned along his journey. He watched as his students' eyes sparkled with excitement and their talents flourished under his guidance.

Elion understood that success is not measured solely by external achievements but by the impact we have on those around us. He had once thought success tasted solely sweet, but now he knew that true success had a bittersweet flavor, reminding us of the sacrifices made and the lessons learned along the way.

In Willow Creek, Elion found fulfillment and contentment. He still performed in small local venues, enchanting his audience with his music, but his primary focus was on nurturing the next generation of musicians and ensuring they held on to their love for music.

And as he watched his students blossom, Elion knew that even though success may be bittersweet, the journey toward it could be just as beautiful, if not more so.

THE UNITY IN DIVERSITY

In a small town called Harmonyville, there lived a group of friends who were as different as could be. Each friend had their own quirks, talents, and dreams, yet they all shared a deep bond that made them feel like they were part of something truly special.

First, there was Emma, a bookworm who could spend hours lost in fantasy worlds. She had an insatiable curiosity and a love for knowledge that inspired her friends to explore the world with an open mind.

Then there was Max, a budding musician with a heart full of passion and melodies. His guitar chords and soulful lyrics brought warmth and harmony to the group, reminding them of the power of music to connect people.

Sara was a natural-born leader, always organizing events and bringing people together. Her charisma and boundless energy made her the glue that held the group together, ensuring that everyone felt included and valued.

On the other hand, there was Ethan, a quiet and introspective artist. He saw the world through a different lens, capturing beauty in the simplest of moments and teaching his friends to appreciate the little things that often go unnoticed.

And then there was Lily, a free-spirited adventurer who lived life with a sense of wild abandon. She constantly pushed the boundaries, encouraging her friends to step out of their comfort zones and embrace the unknown.

Despite their differences, these friends cherished their unique qualities and saw the beauty in their individuality. They celebrated each other's successes, supported each other through challenges, and always found a way to meet in the middle.

In the end, it was their shared values that brought them together - kindness, acceptance, and a genuine love for one another. They believed that even though they were different, they could still create a harmonious world where everyone's strengths were celebrated and weaknesses were supported.

And so, in the small town of Harmonyville, this group of friends taught the world a valuable lesson - that unity can be found even among the most diverse individuals. They showed that when people come together, embracing their differences while celebrating their similarities, incredible things can happen. They proved that being different yet the same can create a bond that is unbreakable, and a friendship that lasts a lifetime.

THE NIGHT DREAM

Alice had a night dream about superficial heroes. She was standing in a deserted city square surrounded by tall buildings, their facades glinting in the sunlight. In the center of the square, there was an old stone fountain, and standing atop it were two figures who were obviously supposed to be superheroes.

Alice stared at them, puzzled. They wore bright, gaudy costumes; brightly-coloured tights, capes, and masks, and their faces were hidden behind flashy masks.

However, Alice could see something beneath their costumes. Their eyes wereexpressionless, their mouths were downturned, and there was an aura of sadness about them. It seemed like they weren't really heroic at all, but rather a parody of heroes.

Alice awoke with a start. It felt as though she had seen a clown version of heroism. But she was still troubled by how empty the superheroes in her dream had seemed despite their flashy costumes. It seemed as though they were trying to pretend to be heroic, but weren't able to achieve true heroism.

Alice wasn't sure if her dream had any deeper meaning or was just a silly dream, but it made her think. It taught her that heroism isn't about the costume or the flash, but about having heart and genuine courage.

Liz had always dreamed of going to the World of Emotions. Everyone told her it was impossible—a made-up place, a mere fairy tale in the minds of children like her. But nothing could stop her from envisioning a magical kingdom of feelings.

One day, a mysterious letter arrived for her. It said: 'Make your dream come true, and go to the World of Emotions'. She was overjoyed, and quickly packed her bags and set off on her journey.

The World of Emotions was like nothing Liz could ever have imagined. Everywhere she looked there was an emotion waiting to be explored. There were Joy Hills and Sad Valleys, filled with bursts of laughter and tears that ran for miles. There were Harmony Forests, Sweet Lakes, and Heat Plains, where the air crackled with glee and the sun shone brightly.

She explored each place with all her senses. She tasted the love in chocolate-covered-strawberry meadows and heard the anger in the echoing roar of thunder. She felt the peace of the sun-soaked fields and the warmth of a gentle embrace. Everywhere she went, the World of Emotions revealed something new.

On her last night in the World of Emotions, Liz finally understood what made it special. All around, in every corner, she could feel the connection between all the feelings—how sadness could lead to joy, how hate could be made beautiful through love, how compassion and understanding create harmony.

Liz left the World of Emotions with a new appreciation for all the emotions that make us human. She would never forget the lessons she learned there, and vowed to always show gratitude and kindness to all those around her.

THE CHAT OF TEARS WITH EYES

Years ago, in a land far away, there existed a magical forest called Tearhaven. Within Tearhaven, there lived a mysterious creature known as Tears with Eyes. These creatures were unlike any other, for they were sentient tears that could see and communicate with one another through a unique form of telepathy. Their emotions were so intense that they could convey entire stories with just a single tear.

In the heart of Tearhaven stood a majestic willow tree, known as the Wisdom Willow. Legend had it that the Wisdom Willow had the power to grant one wish to whoever could decipher its complex riddle. Many tears had attempted to solve the riddle, but none had succeeded. However, there was one tear, named Willow, who possessed a determination like no other.

Willow was a special tear, said to have been born from the laughter of a moonlit night. Her translucent teardrop shape was adorned with twinkling stars, and her empathetic nature made her the most sought after companion for any tear seeking solace. But Willow desired more than just comforting others; she longed for knowledge and the power to unlock the secrets of the Wisdom Willow.

One fateful day, Willow overheard a conversation among the wind spirits whispering about the enigmatic riddle of the Wisdom Willow. Intrigued, she decided to venture deep into the forest to seek the truth.

As she trudged through the dense foliage, she encountered a group of Tears with Eyes engaged in a heated argument. They were discussing the nature of their existence and questioning whether they truly belonged in this world or if they were just figments of imagination. Willow, being consumed by her curiosity, decided to approach them.

"Dear Tears, why do you doubt your own existence?" she asked gently. "We possess the power to convey emotions and stories through our tears. Our presence is evidence enough that we are real, sentient beings."

The Tears with Eyes hushed their bickering and looked at Willow intently, as if finally realizing the truth she spoke. Together, they decided to unite their tears to solve the riddle of the Wisdom Willow.

Days turned into weeks, and weeks into months as Willow and the Tears with Eyes tirelessly deciphered the riddle. They immersed themselves in ancient lore, sought the guidance of forest spirits, and studied the patterns of moonlight filtering through the willow branches. Their efforts were not in vain, for slowly but surely, they unraveled the mystical words of the riddle.

One misty morning, as the sun gleamed through the branches, Willow stood before the Wisdom Willow, reciting the riddle with newfound confidence. "In the depths of your sorrow and the shimmer of your joy, lies the wisdom that can mend or destroy. With tears that see beyond the veil of lies, reveal to me the truth that underlies."

Suddenly, the willow tree came alive, its branches gracefully swaying as if applauding Willow's triumph. With a gentle breeze, the Wisdom Willow whispered, "You have proven your worth, young tear. What is your deepest desire?"

Without hesitation, Willow replied, "I wish for the gift of eternal knowledge and the power to create understanding between all beings."

Upon hearing her wish, the Wisdom Willow bestowed a silver teardrop pendant upon Willow, signifying her newfound wisdom. As she donned the pendant, she felt a surge of energy coursing through her translucent form.

From that day forth, Willow became the voice of reason and empathy in Tearhaven. She used her newfound wisdom to help others understand the true nature of their emotions, bridging gaps of misunderstanding and bringing harmony to their lives.

But Willow's journey didn't end there. She often returned to the Wisdom Willow, engaging in deep conversations about the secrets of the universe, the meaning of life, and the intricate web of connections binding all living beings. And during those conversations, her teardrop eyes sparkled with both the weight of wisdom and the lightness of endless possibilities.

And so, tear by tear, Tearhaven evolved into a place of understanding, compassion, and unity. Thanks to Willow's unwavering determination and the power of her tears, the Tears with Eyes discovered the greatness that lay within them and, in doing so, transformed their world forever. The story of Willow and the Wisdom Willow became legend, echoing through the ages as a testament to the enduring power of tears and the beauty of seeking knowledge.

Once upon a time, in a small village nestled at the foot of towering mountains, there lived a young adventurer named Ethan. Ethan was always yearning for excitement and thrills that lay beyond the boundaries of his mundane village life. He dreamt of exploring far-off lands and uncovering hidden treasures. One day, his dream was about to come true when he stumbled upon an ancient map in the attic of his family's old farmhouse.

The map depicted a mystical desert called the Sands of Enigma. Legends whispered that this desert held secrets beyond imagination, but only the bravest of souls could hope to unravel its mysteries. The moment Ethan laid eyes on that faded parchment, he knew that his true adventure was waiting in the Sands of Enigma.

Equipped with his trusty backpack, compass, and a sense of unwavering determination, Ethan bid farewell to his family and set out on his quest. The journey to the Sands of Enigma was treacherous, requiring him to traverse dense jungles, cross treacherous rivers, and climb up jagged cliffs. With each step, Ethan could feel his heart racing with anticipation.

Finally, after weeks of grueling travel, he arrived at the edge of a vast desert shimmering under the scorching sun. As he entered the Sands of Enigma, Ethan noticed that the very air seemed to crackle with magic. The sand dunes stretched endlessly in every direction, concealing secrets that only the chosen few could uncover.

Ethan navigated through the desert's unforgiving terrain, facing fierce sandstorms and dune avalanches along the way. Each challenge only fueled his determination further, as he knew that the true treasure lay just beyond his reach. As he ventured deeper into this enchanted landscape, he encountered peculiar creatures never before seen by human eyes. There were sand serpents with golden scales, soaring sandbirds with wings of fire, and even mischievous sand sprites who played pranks on unsuspecting travellers.

One fateful night, while camping under a starlit sky, Ethan discovered a hidden oasis tucked away amidst the vast expanse of sand. The oasis held a majestic temple, guarded by statues that seemed to come to life as he approached. At the heart of the temple, he found a shimmering portal, pulsating with an otherworldly glow.

Ethan knew in his heart that this was the moment he had been seeking. He bravely stepped through the portal, unsure of what awaited him on the other side. To his astonishment, he found himself in an ancient city bathed in a warm, golden light. The city was populated by wise sages, who held the key to unraveling the secrets of the Sands of Enigma.

Under the guidance of the sages, Ethan explored forgotten libraries filled with ancient scrolls and consulted mystic seers who revealed glimpses of the desert's true power. He discovered that the Sands of Enigma possessed the ability to grant incredible powers to those who proved themselves worthy. Only those with pure intentions and a heart full of kindness could harness this power for good.

Ethan spent months immersing himself in the teachings of the sages, honing his skills, and mastering the art of sand manipulation. He uncovered ancient rituals and secret spells, transforming himself into a formidable warrior with power over the desert itself.

Armed with newfound abilities, Ethan returned to his hometown, but he was no longer the wide-eyed adventurer who had set out months ago. He became a protector, using his powers to defend the villagers from any danger that came their way. He was no longer just a dreamer; he had become a hero.

And so, the legend of Ethan, the adventurer of the Sands of Enigma, was etched into the annals of history. His tale inspired generations of young dreamers, showing them that true adventure awaits those who have the courage to chase their dreams and embrace the unknown. The Sands of Enigma may have been an unforgettable chapter in Ethan's life, but his journey had only just begun.

THE DEMON WITHIN

In the older era, in the enchanted kingdom of Eldoria, there lived a young woman named Elara. She possessed a pure heart and was beloved by all who knew her. But little did anyone suspect that deep within Elara's heart resided a hidden demon, a secret that haunted her every breath.

Elara had always felt a dark presence lingering within her soul, and as the years passed, its power grew stronger. The demon reveled in her moments of vulnerability, using fear, doubt, and anger to slowly consume her from within.

As Elara ventured through the forest one moonlit night, she stumbled upon an ancient tome that promised to reveal the truth behind her inner demons. Eager for answers, she began to decipher the mystical words. Unbeknownst to her, the book was a conduit to a realm where demons and mythical creatures resided.

With every page turn, Elara's heart beat faster, pounding with anticipation and curiosity.

Suddenly, she found herself transported to an unknown realm, shrouded in darkness. The only source of light came from an ethereal being standing before her – a spirit who identified himself as Azrael.

Azrael was a wise and ancient guide, who had watched over Elara since she was born. He explained that the demon dwelling within her heart had been trapped there long ago, a punishment for an ancestor's misdeeds. As generations passed, the demon's power grew, waiting for the perfect moment to strike.

Elara was desperate for a solution, longing to rid herself of this malevolent entity. Azrael revealed that the only way to expel the demon was to embark on a perilous journey through the treacherous Abyss of Shadows. The journey would test her strength, resolve, and faith, but victory would bring her the freedom she sought.

With her heart trembling yet determined, Elara agreed to the challenge and embarked on her quest. The Abyss of Shadows was a foreboding place, filled with twisted creatures and devious illusions. Elara had to rely on her intuition and inner strength to traverse the treacherous path.

As she delved deeper into the Abyss, Elara encountered manifestations of her own fears and insecurities. The demon within her heart manipulated these illusions, trying to tempt her into surrendering her resolve. But Elara, fueled by her unwavering desire for liberation, resisted the demon's temptations and mustered the courage to press forward.

Days turned into weeks, and Elara's determination only grew stronger. She encountered allies along the way, each with their own demons to confront. Together, they supported one another through the darkest of trials, reminding each other of their worth and the strength that resided within.

Finally, after what felt like an eternity, Elara reached the heart of the Abyss. It was a place of profound darkness where the demon's power was at its apex. With a surge of determination, Elara confronted the demon, her voice filled with unwavering conviction.

"Be gone, foul creature! No longer shall you haunt my heart. I am Elara, and I refuse to be shackled by your darkness! Release me from your grip!"

The demon's malevolent laugh echoed through the chamber, attempting to intimidate Elara once more. But she stood strong, refusing to let fear guide her actions any longer.

Drawing upon her inner strength, Elara unleashed a blinding light from within her heart. It was a light so pure and radiant that it banished the demon's darkness in an instant. Its cries of anguish filled the abyss, fading into nothingness.

With the demon vanquished, Elara found herself transported back to Eldoria, her home. The villagers were in awe of her transformation. Elara, previously burdened by the demon within, now radiated with a newfound light and strength. She became a beacon of hope, showing others that even the darkest of battles can be won.

From that day forward, Elara devoted her life to helping others conquer and confront their inner demons, becoming a renowned healer and counselor. Her story spread far and wide, inspiring generations to embrace their own darkness and find the strength to overcome.

And so, the tale of Elara, the girl who defeated the demon within her heart, lived on as a reminder that no matter how formidable our internal struggles may be, we all possess the power to triumph over the darkest of forces – if only we believe in ourselves.

www.ingramcontent.com/pod-product-compliance
Lightning Source LLC
La Vergne TN
LVHW090124160826
845673LV00015B/840

* 9 7 9 8 8 9 1 3 3 5 0 0 4 *